Enchantment of the World

SINGAPORE

By Marion Marsh Brown

Consultant for Singapore: Clark D. Neher, Ph.D., Chairman, Department of Political Science, Northern Illinois University, DeKalb, Illinois

Consultant for Reading: Robert L. Hillerich, Ph.D., Bowling Green State University, Bowling Green, Ohio

CHILDRENS PRESS ®
CHICAGO

Seiwaen Gardens, one of the largest Japanese gardens outside of Japan

Library of Congress Cataloging-in-Publication Data

Brown, Marion Marsh.
  Singapore / by Marion Marsh Brown.
    p.   cm. — (Enchantment of the world)
  Includes index.
  Summary: Discusses the history, geography, people, and
culture of the island republic which is Asia's smallest
independent state, yet plays a major political and
economic role in the East.
  ISBN 0-516-02715-8
  1. Singapore—Juvenile literature. [1. Singapore.]
I. Title. II. Series.
DS598.S7B76 1989
959.57—dc20

89-34280
CIP
AC

Picture Acknowledgments
AP/Wide World Photos, Inc.: 21, 23 (2 photos), 108
© **Cameramann International, Ltd.:** 6, 10, 24, 26 (3
photos), 28 (2 photos), 29, 30, 31, 32, 35, 37 (2 photos), 38
(2 photos), 40, 42, 43, 45 (left), 46 (2 photos), 47 (2 photos),
48 (2 photos), 50, 51, 53, 54 (2 photos), 56 (2 photos), 58,
60, 62, 63, 65, 66 (2 photos), 67, 68, 71 (2 photos), 72, 74 (2
photos), 76 (inset), 78, 79, 80, 82, 85, 90 (2 photos), 92, 98,
101, 102, 105, 109, 111 (2 photos)
The Granger Collection, New York: 15
Historical Pictures Service, Chicago: 16
© **Emilie Lepthien:** 87 (2 photos)
North Wind Picture Archives: 13
© **Photri:** 59
Shostal Associates: © J. David Day: 4, 20 (right), 45 (right)
Tom Stack & Associates: © Sheryl S. McNee: 8
Tony Stone Worldwide: © Dave Saunders: Cover; © Robin
Smith: 76; © Michael Feeney: 110
Third Coast Stock Source: © Ted H. Funk: 5, 34, 41, 44, 120
Valan: © Christine Osborne: 52, 61
**Courtesy Flag Research Center, Winchester,
Massachusetts 01890:** Flag on back cover
Cover: Central Business District and Harbor

Chinese-owned produce markets are found throughout Singapore.

TABLE OF CONTENTS

Chapter 1
UNIQUE SINGAPORE

Singapore. Is it an island, a city, or a state? Surprisingly, this exotic sounding name applies to all three. Singapore is a Southeast Asian island, a small republic, and a big, bustling, beautiful city all in one. The island republic, the smallest in its part of the world, is unique in that the majority of its two-and-a-half million people live in the city that people usually think of when they hear the word Singapore.

The word sounds exciting and romantic, and the story of its origin fulfills expectations. The name, so the story goes, dates back to the twelfth century when an adventurous Sumatran prince named Sri Tri Bauna came to the island, which was a part of his realm, to hunt. While he was stalking wild animals in the jungle that covered the island at that time, one of them turned on him in a ferocious attack. Sri Tri Bauna's attendants came to his rescue and the prince's life was saved.

Later his men reported that a lion had made the attack, although it is believed today that the beast was a tiger, for the woods were full of them until relatively recent times. Nevertheless, it was the reported lion in this dramatic incident that gave Singapore her name, derived from *Singa Pura*, which in the Malay language means "Lion City."

Opposite page: New Bridge Road, one of the main streets in Chinatown

Singapore is a crowded city, even away from the central business district.

While a bit of the jungle that the prince would have found on the island eight hundred years ago still remains, most of the "jungle" today is one of concrete and skyscrapers, constituting one of Asia's biggest, busiest, and most colorful cities—teeming with activity from pedibike rickshaws to Mercedes on her streets and from sampans to yachts and international freighters in her waters.

The people on her streets and docks are as interestingly diverse as her vehicles and vessels.

SMALLEST STATE

Singapore is Asia's smallest independent state. The island is only 26-miles (42-kilometers) long and 14-miles (23-kilometers) wide, and slightly over 238 square miles (616 square kilometers) in area. This means it is about one-fourth the size of Long Island, New York, or a little larger than Guam in the Mariana Island group in the Pacific Ocean. The area of Singapore does not remain constant, however, because frequent landfill is added when more space is needed for buildings.

Singapore is situated in the South China Sea, just off the southern tip of the Malay Peninsula. The island and the peninsula are so close together that they are joined by a causeway scarcely 1 mile (1.6 kilometers) in length.

Singapore's uniqueness in the world picture lies in the fact that she is only a very small island, physically, yet plays a major part in the East politically and economically.

HOT, HUMID, AND LUXURIANT

As Singapore is only 87 miles (140 kilometers) north of the equator, it has no marked change of seasons; the average temperature the year around is 80 degrees Fahrenheit (26.7 degrees Celsius).

Because it is surrounded by the sea and annually receives from 75 to 100 inches (127 to 254 centimeters) of rain, Singapore steams in the sun. Humidity is often very high.

Such conditions are favorable for lush tropical growth, both in the sandy earth along the waterfront and in the marshy land elsewhere. Flowers, shrubs, and trees grow luxuriantly both inside and outside the city, and blooming plants furnish a kaleidoscope of bright colors against the backdrop of dark-green forest.

Some outlying areas are still covered with the native growth of the jungle. Many of these areas, however, have been cleared and are now small, neat cultivated farms.

Sentosa, an island south of the mainland

OFFSHORE ISLANDS

The state of Singapore includes, beside the island with its renowned city, over fifty tiny nearby islands, mere dots on the sea. Many of these are uninhabited and are so small that they are referred to as islets, but a few have been developed for industrial sites.

DIAMONDLIKE

Singapore island is diamond shaped. In other ways than its shape, it is also a diamond: a diamond in the sea, sparkling with bright lights at night, and a gem of great value to the world because of its important port, the second largest in the world.

Chapter 2

CURIOUS BEGINNINGS

According to geologists, the island of Singapore was once joined to the Malay Peninsula. Thus it is not surprising that the early history of Singapore is blended with that of present-day Malaysia.

From the seventh to the eleventh century, there is little recorded history of the area. The first written reference to Singapore appeared in Chinese chronicles of the fourteenth century. However, oral history handed down over the centuries tells of the existence of a settlement called *Temasek* (Sea Town) on the south coast of the island several hundred years prior to this time. The "Sea Town" boasted a walled fortress and its inhabitants were fishermen. They had a small trade with passing vessels, but the important cargo ships going to and from Canton, China, paid them little heed as they sailed by.

It is quite probable that the famous traveler Marco Polo saw this settlement as he passed through the Strait of Malacca in 1284.

Had he been some years later, however, he would not have seen any people, for by the end of the fourteenth century the settlement had been completely wiped out by a warring Malay kingdom from the island of Java. Yet like the fabled Phoenix, the Sea Town was destined to "rise from the ashes," and by the time another hundred years had passed, the tip of the island was again inhabited, only to be captured (though not decimated), along with the Malay Peninsula, by Portugal.

For the next three hundred years, the lot of the Malay Peninsula and the island of Singapore was bounced about like a rubber ball. From Portuguese rule, the country went to the Dutch; from the Dutch to the British; and then back to the Dutch.

Finally, in 1811, Singapore was annexed to the Malay Sultanate of Johore. A prince of this house, called the *Temenggong*, became chief of the island.

THE EAST INDIA COMPANY

At this time the major European nations—Denmark, The Netherlands, France, and England—were in competition for trade in the East Indies. This was a very lucrative trade. Each of these countries had established its own East India Company. Ships from India plied the seas carrying valuable cargo, like silk and opium, to such distant points as China and Japan. Each East India Company had offices in its homeland.

YOUNG THOMAS STAMFORD RAFFLES

England had its home offices in London in a handsome building called East India House, and here worked a fourteen-year-old boy, Thomas Stamford Raffles. He held a position as clerk. He was to play a significant part in Singapore's future.

When Raffles's father lost his fortune, Thomas was forced to leave the boarding school he had been attending and seek employment. It was with the East India Company that he found it.

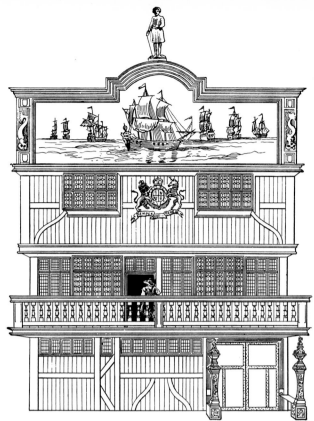

The old East India House, headquarters of the East India Company

Two years after Thomas took the position as clerk, his father died, and Thomas became the sole support of his mother and five sisters. For ten years he held the same position, with little increase in salary. At the same time a man who was to become famous in English literature also was employed there as a clerk—Charles Lamb.

During the years Thomas was a clerk, he did much more than fulfill the duties of the job. Every leisure moment he spent in educating himself. He was a very bright young man who was intensely curious about many things. He read widely, taking notes on what he read. He learned a second language, French.

His supervisors took note of his unusual industry, his ability, and eventually of his extensive knowledge. The head of the office, William Ramsey, became his friend and invited him to his home where he met socially prominent and politically influential people.

RAFFLES MOVES EAST

After ten years, the ambitious young man's big opportunity arrived. In 1805 the East India Company of England established a trading post on the island of Penang, off the west coast of the Malay Peninsula. Thomas Stamford Raffles was chosen to go to this post as assistant to the secretary. He was then twenty-four years old.

Not only did the young man's salary take a giant leap, his promotion was the first step toward the leading role he was to play in the story of Singapore.

Even before he reached Penang, Raffles had learned the Malay language that was spoken there, and on arrival he began an extensive study of the culture, the history, and the flora and fauna of the area. He was a personable young man, warm and friendly, and he soon made friends with men in high places who were located in various stations in Southeast Asia, and even in India.

Lord Minto, governor-general of the company in India, became his mentor. Through such contacts, plus his wide knowledge and notable ability, Raffles soon had taken another step toward Singapore. He was made governor of Java, another island in the Malay Archipelago. He was a benevolent and soon a beloved ruler. In 1817 he was knighted by King George III of Great Britain and was thereafter known as Sir Stamford Raffles. As his influence in Southeast Asia increased, he was given even wider power and responsibility.

At this time the Dutch East India Company was making great inroads into the India trade. England badly needed to establish a station of her company that would prevent the Dutch interference. Raffles recommended that a trading post be established on one of

An oil painting of Sir Thomas Stamford Raffles

the islands lying off the point of the Malay Peninsula. Such a port would command the passage from the Indian Ocean to the China Sea. He further noted that such a move needed to be made soon, before the Dutch beat the English to the draw.

Raffles was given the power to attempt such a settlement, as long as the Dutch should not be aroused to military action against the British. He had a certain island in mind for this new post of the English East India Company, an island named Singapore.

RAFFLES'S COUP

In a small merchant ship, *The Indiana*, Raffles set sail for the island of Singapore to carry out what proved to be the coup of the century.

He had learned before leaving for the island that it was under the Sultanate of Johore. He had further learned of the death of the

*Sultans ruled Johore
during the
nineteenth century.*

sultan some six years before and of the contention between his two eldest sons over succession to the throne. The elder, Tunku Long, had not been at home at the time of his father's death, and by the time he had returned to Johore (transport by sailing ship was very slow) he found that his younger brother, who had been acting as regent, refused to step down. Still, as Raffles well knew, Tunku Long was the rightful heir to the throne.

On January 28, 1819, Raffles anchored off the sandy beaches of Singapore. Going ashore, he found a hundred or so thatch-roofed huts along the banks of the Singapore River, otherwise mangrove swamps and dense jungle.

He sent word to the Temenggong that he wished to call on him and received in return a cordial invitation for the following day. When the two men met, as soon as introductory formalities were over, Raffles went directly to the point: He wished to lease the island of Singapore for the East India Company of England.

The Temenggong replied that he did not have the authority to make such a transaction. It would take the consent of the sultan of Johore. Raffles of course knew this, and knowing that the acting sultan was not the legitimate heir to the throne, he sent for Tunku Long, the elder brother, who was residing on the small island of Bulang, not far away.

Tunku Long responded to Raffles's summons immediately, arriving in Singapore the very next day, February 1. Even before his arrival, Raffles had persuaded the Temenggong to make a temporary agreement allowing him to bring his men ashore and set up a post. So when Tunku Long arrived, a company of soldiers was tented on the island, and a crude hut had been erected for Raffles.

When Raffles explained to Tunku Long his plan to make him sultan of Johore, the prince was at first hesitant. He was not a particularly brave man and he feared his brother who was holding the throne and the Dutch who were backing him. Raffles's persuasiveness, however, plus his promise of military support if it should be needed, won the prince over.

On February 6, an imposing ceremony was held on the island, crowning Tunku Long sultan of Johore. Even the traditional red carpet was laid, leading to the ceremonial tent. The ceremony was climaxed by a salute from the guns of the troops Raffles had brought with him.

Having been named sultan, Tunku Long signed the agreement that Raffles had drawn up, giving possession of the island of Singapore to the English East India Company. Raffles had brought off the coup.

Tunku Long was to receive five thousand Spanish dollars a year from the East India Company and would be protected by the British against any outside interference.

AFTER THE COUP

Raffles hoisted the British flag, the Union Jack. He ordered his men to build a fort for protection, appointed William Farquhar resident commandant, set up rules for keeping records, laid out a plan for city streets, and after one week departed from the island he had set on its way to becoming one of East Asia's brightest stars.

Singapore was to be a free port, and very soon cargo ships were stopping at the island and trade became lively. Population grew, as did the money in the coffers of the English East India Company and in those of the colonists.

The only major problem in the early years of Singapore's takeoff to success was that pirates looted the ships in her nearby waters. In 1832 four Chinese ships belonging to Chinese residents of the island set out on a concerted attack on the pirate ships, hoping to put an end to the problem. Although they were not completely successful, they were able to discourage a major portion of the pirates, and this helped boost Singapore's rapid rise.

In the late nineteenth century, a large wave of immigrants from South China added greatly to the population and helped balance the proportion of Chinese and Malays. Other races were to come, however. Indians and Europeans, including the British, and a smattering of other Asians, including Indonesians and Thais, arrived. Singapore rapidly grew into a multiracial metropolis and state.

Chapter 3

THE TWENTIETH CENTURY—DRAMA AND CHANGE

By the beginning of the twentieth century, the sleepy little village of but 100 inhabitants had become a bustling port city of over 200,000, and its citizens no longer thought of themselves as Malays, Chinese, or Indians, but as Singaporeans.

On the main route between India and China, a continual parade of tall-masted ships entered and left her port. From these ships was unloaded rich cargo to be stored temporarily in Singapore, then distributed to other Southeast Asian countries. Also the island port became a distribution point for manufactured goods from the West.

But during those years, Great Britain had made some important moves involving Singapore. In 1867 she had combined Singapore with Penang and Malacca (nearby Malayan settlements) to form a crown colony known as the Straits Settlements. Singapore was still a part of this combined colony during the years of World War II.

Because they could not be turned, the big guns at the naval station could not protect Singapore when the Japanese invaded during World War II.

Furthermore, Great Britain had built an imposing naval base called an "Island Fortress," on the north shore of Singapore, which had taken twenty years to complete. She was preparing to protect her valuable colony at any price.

WAR

Then came World War II, which was to test this "fortress" and find it wanting.

The war, initiated in 1939 when Germany invaded Poland, had taken on global proportions by 1941, when Japan made her surprise strike on Pearl Harbor, Hawaii. In Japan's overall plan of "attack and destroy," Malaya and Singapore were soon to follow Pearl Harbor.

Fearing some such action, England had sent two of her prize battleships, the *Enterprise* and the *Prince of Wales*, to guard the

In 1942, a Japanese officer escorts the British military to talks
in preparation to surrendering Singapore to her Japanese captors.

harbor at Singapore. But just two days after the attack on Pearl Harbor, Japanese planes flew over those ships and torpedoed and sank them.

Still, there was the naval station, its big implanted guns turned on the harbor. Surely they could turn back any attacking force.

But instead of coming by sea as anticipated, the Japanese, 100,000 strong, came by land, down the Malaysian Peninsula and across the causeway. The big guns at the naval station, pointed out to sea, could not be turned. The island's defense lay with the British land troops that numbered less than half those of the enemy. Stationed around the perimeter of the island, they made a thin line of defense.

Singapore could not be saved. A week after the invasion began, late in the afternoon of February 15, General Arthur Percival, commander of the British forces, met General Tomoyuki Yamashita under a flag of truce and surrendered.

JAPANESE OCCUPATION

The Singaporeans, ill prepared for the assault on their homeland, had suffered greatly, and now they were under occupation by the Japanese. The name of Singapore was changed to *Shonan*, Japanese for "City of Light," and many other changes took place. No longer was there money flowing from the shipping industry. The Singaporeans knew fear and privation.

For three-and-a-half years, until the Japanese surrendered to the Allied Forces in September of 1945, the Japanese flag flew over Government House.

RAPID CHANGE

At the end of World War II, Singapore, with the other members of the Straits Settlements, was returned to Great Britain. In 1946, however, the Straits Settlements was dissolved, and the island of Singapore became a separate crown colony.

As early as 1955, the crown allowed her partial self-government, with the people electing their representative legislature. But the Singaporeans were becoming restive under Britain, and in 1959 the mother country granted them complete internal self-government. It was at this time that Lee Kuan Yew first became prime minister.

It was still believed, at least by Great Britain, that Singapore was not strong enough to be a separate state. The objective at the time was to make her a part of a then-forming Malay federation. This was accomplished, and on September 16, 1963, a new nation, of which Singapore was a part, was proclaimed. It was called Malaysia.

Above: Officials gathered in the conference room in Singapore's Municipal Building on September 14, 1945 to witness the complete surrender of the Japanese, ending World War II. Right: Celebrating the Malaysia Federation in 1964

Singapore, however, was not to remain a part of the new nation for long. The Singaporeans feared domination by Malays, and very soon political and economic disputes arose. In the summer of 1964, riots broke out on the streets of Singapore between Malays and Chinese, and sharp-worded arguments between leaders followed.

As a result of this dissension, Singapore withdrew on August 9, 1965. It was then that Singapore became an independent sovereign state.

In less than 150 years, this strategic tropical island had gone from a trading post to a republic.

SELF-GOVERNMENT

The government of the new republic followed the lines that the British had set up, with the usual three branches: Executive, Judicial, and Legislative.

The Supreme Court, in the center of the photo

The judicial power is vested in a Supreme Court and the usual subordinate courts: district courts, magistrates' courts, juvenile courts, and small-claims courts.

The Legislative branch, called the Parliament, following British precedent, has seventy-five members, each of whom is elected for a five-year term. It is called a unicameral body, meaning it has just one chamber.

The Executive branch has a president, elected by the Parliament for a period of four years. He, in turn, appoints a prime minister, and together the two name (from the Parliament) a cabinet of fourteen members.

PRIME MINISTER YEW, A FATHER FIGURE

Lee Kuan Yew, an able lawyer of Chinese extraction, became the first prime minister when Singapore was granted her independence in 1965. He was still prime minister in 1989.

This unusual circumstance stems from the fact that the Singapore Constitution suggests that the president appoint a prime minister who "commands the confidence of the majority of the members of Parliament." Lee Kuan Yew is considered the founder of the People's Action party, known as the PAP. It is this party that is in power, with ordinarily some 99 percent of the members of Parliament being of this political party. Lee Kuan Yew, having proved himself with the Parliament, has been reappointed by each president. He is now the world's longest-serving elected prime minister.

Born in Singapore, the son and grandson of wealthy shipowners, Lee Kuan Yew came well prepared to his position of eminence. After graduation from the then-Raffles College in Singapore, he was sent to England where he was enrolled at Oxford to study law. After having received a law degree from Oxford, he furthered his advanced education by going to the United States and taking a degree in administration at Harvard.

In 1950 he set up a law practice in Singapore and two years later became adviser to several trade unions. It was from this work that his political career got its start.

Though brilliant, eloquent, and confident, Lee is basically a quiet, introspective man. He has become a father figure to his people, and they work hard for him, obeying him in small things and large. He exhorts them to brush their teeth, to speak proper Mandarin Chinese, not to spit in the street, and not to drop a cigarette butt or candy wrapper on the sidewalk or street at the cost of a S $500 fine. (One Singapore dollar, S $, equaled 46 United States cents in June 1988.) He demands neatness and expects unity—and he gets it, thereby obtaining for Singapore the epithet of "Lee's tidy little island nation."

Above: Children posing on a motorbike. Below: A teenage Malaysian boy (left) and a young woman (right) in an Indian cultural show.

Chapter 4

THE COLORFUL PEOPLE

Singapore's most interesting feature is her people. The various ethnic groups that make their homes here make an interesting contrast. There are over two-and-a-half million people living on the island. Over three-fourths of the population is made up of ethnic Chinese. Of the remainder, Malays, the first settlers on the island, make up the next largest group, about 15 percent of the total. Indians come next, constituting a little over 6 percent. Beyond these three major ethnic groups, there are smaller numbers of many others: Ceylonese, Vietnamese, Pakistanis, Arabs, Europeans, and Americans.

An unceasing display of colors and a great variety of styles are therefore to be seen in the dress of the people on the streets, especially in Chinatown, Little India, and on Arab Street. Color contrasts abound, from the saffron robes of the Buddhist priests and the silver- and gold-threaded saris of Indian women to the gray garb of Chinese coolies.

Men and women in well-tailored Western-style dress and a jean-clad younger generation bustle among those clad in styles characteristic of their calling: women in long gray skirts, men in

Indian stores (above) and Chinatown (left)

long and short robes, and others in short trousers with long, sashed tunics. White-turbaned heads bob among bare and traditionally hatted heads.

The Singaporeans form a bright and exciting parade on any day of the week, but on festival days, of which there are many, the parades become spectacular.

There are still distinct divisions in the city where the people are primarily of one ethnic derivation, and these are roughly in the same areas originally laid out by Raffles in 1819. It was his belief that the islanders would live more peaceably and happily if they were grouped so that each nationality would have its own community.

It is as a result of this early grouping that there is a Little India, an even more distinct Chinatown, an Arab Street, and areas where mostly British and Europeans live.

Arab Street is home to Muslim Indians and Arabs.

This is not to say that the Singaporeans have racial barriers, that they do not intermarry, that they do not meet in the workplace and on the "uptown" city streets. Nor does it mean that there is dissension between ethnic groups. Under Prime Minister Lee Kuan Yew's leadership, unity has been stressed and differences minimized.

Despite all this, the visitor in the city can distinguish with no difficulty the British area north of the Singapore River, the Chinese area south of the river, Little India, and Arab Street. The differences in the people, in the architecture, in the shops—in the total effect on the senses of smells, sounds, and sights—are pronounced.

There is a very wealthy class of people in Singapore, made up largely of shipping and finance tycoons. Most in this class are Chinese, with some Europeans. Status symbols of this group can

Blocks of government-built apartments house 80 percent of Singapore's citizens.

be seen in the Mercedes on the streets, in million-dollar homes, in Parisian boutiques and beautifully dressed women, and in country clubs.

The majority of the people in Singapore, however, are middle-class citizens who work hard, save diligently, and live in government-built housing. They are a saving people, whose standard of living compared to that of other Asian people is high.

GOVERNMENT-BUILT HOUSING

Four out of every five people on the island live in government-built housing. In the past twenty-five years, a half million homes have been built under the government's housing program. They are in high-rise apartment buildings, with modern facilities. From the street these high rises are bright with what the Singaporeans jokingly call their "national flag": laundry hung on bamboo poles extended from the windows.

Laundry drying on bamboo poles is jokingly called Singapore's national flag.

Units in the housing projects may be rented or purchased, depending on the area. On the average, about 37 percent of a wage earner's salary goes into housing.

A SAVING PEOPLE

In 1955 a compulsory saving scheme, called the Central Provident Fund was set up to insure that upon retirement or inability to work, people would have sufficient funds to take care of their needs.

The Central Provident Fund has two separate accounts for each member: Ordinary and Medisave. Members can use funds from their Ordinary account to buy apartments and to pay insurance on their homes. Otherwise this money may not be drawn upon until the member is fifty-five years of age.

A family picnic

The Medisave account can be drawn on to pay for hospitalization (for total payment in government hospitals, half payment in private ones). After age fifty-five a person is required to retain a certain amount in his Medisave account for health-related problems after retirement. A Minimum Sum Scheme, recently adopted, ensures that members on reaching the age of sixty will have a minimum of S $230 a month.

Not only are the adult Singaporeans a saving people, so are their children. Although not required to put away for the future as their parents are, over 40 percent of primary schoolchildren and over 90 percent of secondary school pupils have savings accounts.

THE FAMILY

There are multifamily apartments available in the high rises, often two apartments that join or open into each other, so that older and younger family members can be of assistance to each other. Often young families need the older generation for baby-sitting. Grandparents live in one apartment, the younger family in the adjoining one, and when both husband and wife of the young family go off to work in the morning (which is common today as many women are employed outside the home), the children are left in good hands. There are also day-care centers for families that do not have this built-in service. These are carefully supervised by the government.

Singaporean families are small, averaging only 1.6 children each. As the population is not reproducing too quickly, there is no campaign for birth control as there is in most Asian countries. In fact, there is some effort being made to encourage three children per family.

EDUCATION

Although education is not compulsory in Singapore, it is a highly prized opportunity, and over 70 percent of school-age children are in school.

The state boasts a high literacy level, with 86 percent of the population being literate.

One-fourth of the state budget goes to education. Although education is termed "free," parents pay an average of S $10 to 15 a month for "extras" for each child attending school.

Preceding the primary school, which covers first through sixth grade, there are two years of kindergarten available.

At the third-grade level, pupils are "tracked" into slow and fast groups.

Because of the city's multiracial makeup, multilingual programs are necessary. Even in primary school, a pupil studies not only his

A classroom in St. Joseph's School, a private school

own language (Chinese, Malay, or Tamil), but also English. There are four official languages in Singapore: English, Chinese, Malay, and Tamil.

There is a set curriculum for the primary schools that includes mathematics, science studies, and moral education, as well as language.

There are primary schools in every housing area, each accompanied by an adequate playground. In situations where both a primary and a secondary school are housed in adjoining or nearby buildings, more extensive athletic grounds may include a pool, a track, and squash courts.

In order to enter secondary school, students must pass the Primary-School-Leaving-Examination. Results of this examination also are used to track those who pass into the three levels.

Secondary schools are four-year schools, and at the end of the

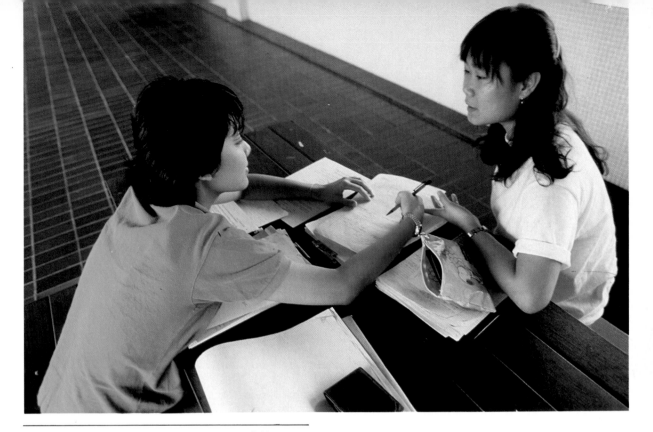

Students at the University of Singapore

four years, students ranking high enough academically may go on to a two-year, preuniversity course. If a student then attends the university, he still has four years of school ahead of him.

Two highly respected universities in Singapore, the University of Singapore and Nanyang University, were merged in 1980 to form the National University of Singapore. Situated on a 371-acre (150-hectare) campus, it offers degrees in accounting and business administration, arts and social sciences, building and architecture, engineering, medicine, dentistry, and law.

Students wishing other specialties can find schools offering such diverse subjects as dance, art, and polytechnics. In such a high-tech city, many job opportunities are available to those skilled in polytechnics, with the result that at any given time some twenty thousand students are enrolled in the two polytechnic schools in Singapore.

Advanced education is heavily subsidized, with government funds paying up to 90 percent of a student's cost of a university education and over 90 percent of one in a polytechnic school.

Agencies other than the government are involved in providing education for the disabled. These include the Singapore Association for the Blind, Singapore Association for the Deaf, the Spastics Children Association, and the Movement for the Intellectually Disabled. These schools are run with volunteer help and are supported by the local Community Chest and the ministry of community development. The ministry of education aids the programs by securing trained teachers for these specialized schools.

There are also numerous foreign schools to accommodate the children of people from abroad who are living in Singapore. These include American, Australian, British, French, German, Japanese, and Swiss institutions.

BUSY HANDS

Many hands are occupied in the fashioning of handmade ethnic items. Chinese calligraphers and mask makers turn out their wares in Chinatown. Idol carvers and makers of temple goods are also at work. Then there are those who make paper items, small houses and cars, to be burned at funerals.

In Little India women fashion beautiful saris and garlands of real flowers to be sold in the shops, where over the doorways hang strings of dried mango leaves, an Indian sign of blessing. Men make leather sandals, belts, and purses, many hand tooled with intricate designs.

On Arab Street the handicraft of Malays appears in handwoven

At the Singapore Handicraft Center,
an artist works on an Oriental
carpet (above) and another artist
finishes a brush and finger painting (left).

baskets of every size, shape, and design. Necessities for a
pilgrimage to Mecca show the dedicated workmanship of
Muslims. These include headdresses, *hajj* caps (special caps that
can be worn only by those who have been to Mecca), scarves,
money belts, and jewel-bright prayer rugs.

There is one area known as the New Ming Village where
porcelain masterpieces of the Ming and Qing period of ancient
China are being recreated in the age-old traditional way. Each
piece, many of which are large vases nearly as tall as the Chinese-
Singaporean who is working on them, is hand decorated with

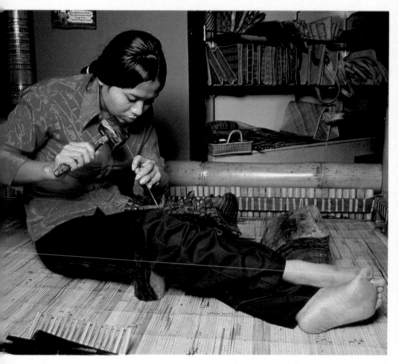

A young woman doing detailed wood carving (left)
and a man working with rosewood (right)

faithful reproductions of the calligraphy and figures in the design
of the original. Once completed, the pieces are for sale—at very
high prices.

Not only the men and women of the older generation are
involved in turning out handicrafts illustrative of their particular
culture, but young people are learning the skills of craft making
indigenous to their race. There are four handicrafts training
centers in Singapore, a part of the government's total education
program. Growing out of this training is the Singapore Handicraft
Center where handmade items from the various cultures of the
island are displayed and sold.

Chapter 5

CULTURE AND
RECREATION

There are plenty of cultural options for the Singaporeans: the Singapore Symphony (one of the world's youngest, founded in 1979); two Chinese orchestras for the Chinese classics, tone poems and folk music; Chinese opera; Sunday evening band concerts in the Botanical Gardens under tall palms; and a unique musical event, a bird-singing concert held on Sunday mornings, where residents in the Jurong area bring their caged birds, hang the cages on poles provided, and then sit back to enjoy the music as each bird tries to outdo its neighbor in trills and songs.

Besides the musical offerings, there is legitimate theater, with plays being staged both in the modern Drama Center and in the gracious old Victoria Theatre. Offerings are amazingly varied, including everything from Malay folk plays and Indian dance dramas to English-language musical comedies.

Traditional Chinese opera is a visual as well as a musical treat.

Going to the cinema is a favorite pastime for Singaporeans, so movie theaters can be found in all areas of the city. English, Chinese, Malay, and Indian movies are shown. Most are subtitled in one or two languages other than the one used in the film.

SPORTS

Both spectator and participator sports are popular in Singapore.

Sports arenas, where a variety of games can be watched, furnish viewing pleasure for thousands. The National Stadium plus nine other arenas provide ample seating and a variety of offerings.

Because of the year-around summer climate, so-called "summer sports" are popular at all times. One weekend in four there is horse racing at the Singapore Turf Club. Four days of every week

The Singapore Polo Club

spectators can watch polo matches at the Singapore Polo Club. There are cricket games every Saturday and Sunday afternoon at the Singapore Cricket Club.

There are spectator water sports, including the Singapore Powerboat Grand Prix in which top powerboat drivers from a half dozen foreign countries participate and the Singapore Dragon Boat Race, which draws rowing teams from many countries.

Among the many participator sports available to the Singaporeans, the ones enjoyed by the largest numbers are badminton, soccer, squash, tennis, and jogging. Rugby is also popular. Golf has fewer participants because most golf courses are at country clubs and they are expensive to join.

Many water sports also are enjoyed: canoeing, waterskiing, surfing, wind surfing, and swimming.

Singaporeans believe in keeping fit, so large numbers take advantage of the many inviting jogging paths, bicycle tracks, and the four "fitness parks" in the city.

*The ferryboat
terminal on
Sentosa Island*

SENTOSA AMUSEMENT PARK

Off the south coast of Singapore Island lies the islet called
Sentosa (Tranquillity). Occupied by British forts during the
colonial period, it has since been developed into a recreation/
amusement park that draws about one million visitors a year.
Having retained much of its natural forest of huge, umbrellalike
trees, the 828-acre (335-hectare) park has a restful, "tranquil" feel,
even though it offers many activities.

To reach Sentosa from the main island, one may take a ferry (a
six-minute ride) or go by cable car from Mt. Faber, one of
Singapore's highest hills at 395 feet (120 meters) above sea level.
The cable-car ride, although only about 1-mile (1.6-kilometer)
long, offers a spectacular view of the city, the harbor, and other
islands to the south.

42

The Surrender Chamber in the Wax Museum

Having been deposited in Sentosa, the visitor has a wide choice of things to do ranging from visiting the Wax Museum, the Maritime Museum, the Coralarium, and the Art Center to roller skating, or swimming and sailing in the lagoon.

The Wax Museum is, in a very realistic fashion, a history museum. Eighty-nine life-size figures depict two surrender ceremonies that occurred during Singapore's involvement in World War II, namely the surrender of the British, who then governed the island, to the Japanese, in 1942, and the surrender of the Japanese to the Allies in 1945. Besides this display, billed as the Surrender Chamber, there is a Pioneers of Singapore exhibit.

The Maritime Museum, though comparatively small, has displays covering the evolution of watercraft, fishing traps and nets, and the history of Singapore's port. By means of models, pictures, and a collection of native crafts, it covers Singapore's connection with the sea.

A map of Singapore made of seashells.

The Coralarium is a unique museum. It not only shows typical coral reefs and structures, different types of coral and how it grows, but also, in an air-conditioned cave, gives viewers the opportunity to see live fluorescent coral.

In addition to coral, the Coralarium features seashells. The total exhibit displays over twenty-five hundred different seashells and types of coral. Exhibits also show how various shells have evolved.

All visitors will surely enjoy the musical fountain that, with its changing sprays, has a synchronized pattern of color changes and musical accompaniment.

The island can be circled by monorail to view the tropical scenery and to stop off at several points of interest if one wishes.

*The crowded night market in Chinatown (left)
is as interesting a diversion as the Lido
nightclub on Orchard Road (right).*

NIGHTLIFE

Singapore is not lacking in nightlife. Enchanting dancers and musicians perform in nightclubs, at hotels, and in dinner theaters. The last named, known in Singapore as theater restaurants, offer lavish cuisine and top-notch shows. Successful Broadway musicals are popular on their entertainment bills.

There are both disco-and-dance establishments and ones for disco only. Some discos have live bands, others, recorded music only; but all are popular among young Singaporeans. One that is unusual offers a high-tech experience, giving the dancers a feeling that they are dancing in space. This effect is produced by the use of a split-level glass floor, mirrors, and imaginative lighting.

Two prewar warehouses along the Singapore River have been converted into Singapore's largest discotheque, with a dance floor that will accommodate four hundred.

A tempting variety of food on display (left) and dried ducks for sale (right)

FOOD, FOOD, FOOD

Probably the favorite recreational activity of Singaporeans is eating out. Opportunities for partaking in this pastime are almost endless, with hundreds of restaurants, bistros, sidewalk cafés, and innumerable "hawker centers" from which to choose.

The variety of food is endless. There is not just one type of Chinese food available, but a number, stemming from the various provinces from which Chinese settlers have emigrated. There are not only Malay dishes to be had, but also a combination of Malay and Chinese known as "nonya," which has developed over the years from families in which Chinese and Malays have intermarried. And there is Indian food of two kinds, northern and southern, with curries the staple for both, but with northern dishes comparatively mild while southern are fiery hot. Also, stemming from Singapore's years as a British colony, there are restaurants specializing in English food. In addition, because of the European settlers and other Asian groups in the city, everything from French to Korean restaurants offer their specialties.

Left: A food vendor cooking at an outdoor stall
Right: A fruit stand adds color to a busy street scene

The most reasonable "eating-out" opportunities are in the hawker centers, which are especially popular with young couples and families. These are most often outdoor stalls, as many as a hundred concentrated in a single area, where vendors do their cooking before the eyes and noses of their customers. The smells of roasting *satay* (meat and fish grilled on skewers over a charcoal fire, then dipped in a sweet peanut sauce), of curries, and of frying noodles beckon the hungry. All the while, hawkers cry their wares, adding to the local color.

DIM SUM

Then there is *dim sum,* a Chinese "must" for those who have an opportunity to sit and sup in mid-morning. Dim sum is the name given to dumplings that are stuffed with various fillings and served with tea. Establishments that feature dim sum are favorite haunts of elderly Chinese men.

The botanic gardens in Seiwaen Gardens (above) and lush bougainvillea flowering outside the home of a wealthy Singaporean (below).

Chapter 6

THE GARDEN CITY

Singapore is often called "The Garden City," and with good reason. Along the multilane expressways, deep pink bougainvillea cascades over walls, while lush green tropical forests provide a dusky backdrop. From balconies of the high rises, bright splashes of color spill from flower boxes.

Then there are the "official" gardens: a Japanese garden and a Chinese garden, beautifully landscaped and manicured. The Japanese garden, Seiwaen (Garden of Tranquillity), is one of the largest outside of Japan. It lives up to its name with its teahouse, its plantings, its bridges, and its stone lanterns. The Chinese garden, on its own small island in a man-made lake, has the charm of old imperial China. It is replete with pagodas, dancing fountains, and lotus ponds.

In the midst of busy shopping centers, unexpected gardens appear. At the Raffles, an oasis of green lies behind the hotel with intriguing paths on which the stroller could be anywhere but in the midst of a towering city.

Beside the intimate, smaller garden and park areas are the forest preserves and other extensive parklands: the Botanical Gardens,

Visitors strolling in the Botanical Gardens

Zoological Gardens, and the Jurong Bird Park. A government board administers these, seeing they are kept neat and beautiful.

BOTANICAL GARDENS

The Botanical Gardens, covering 79 acres (32 hectares), is one of the most beautiful tropical gardens in the world, with more than half a million tropical plants. Tall trees stretch as much as 164 feet (50 meters) into the sky; exotic shrubs, brilliant flowers, and giant ferns all give an authentic picture of Singapore's original natural appearance.

Water lilies and black swans decorate an appealing lake, and there is a spectacular orchid enclosure where 2,600 orchid plants of 250 species bloom in brilliant profusion.

The Botanical Gardens has a claim to fame in that it was here in 1877 that the British director of the gardens, H.N. Ridley, propagated Brazilian rubber plants, which were to be the basis of the extensive Malaysian rubber industry.

This early morning visitor to the Zoological Gardens gets to sit in at breakfast with an orangutan.

AN ANIMAL PARK

The Zoological Gardens furnish a natural setting for over 1,600 animals. The park is neatly landscaped and employs an open-zoo concept, using water and rock walls instead of cages to corral the animals. Some 170 species roam and play here.

This zoo, ranking in the top ten in the world, contains the largest colony of orangutans to be found anywhere and many endangered species: cheetahs, Siberian tigers, clouded leopards, and Malayan tapirs. The world's smallest hoofed animal, the mouse deer, is here also.

Visitors can watch jaguars frolicking in their pool and pumas walking down tree trunks. They can handle a snake, ride an elephant, or pet a lanky giraffe. Twice a day elephants, sea lions, snakes, orangutans, and chimpanzees put on a polished performance, seeming to enjoy the applause of their delighted audience.

Flamingoes in Jurong Bird Park

JURONG BIRD PARK

Even more spectacular than the Botanical and Zoological gardens is the 49-acre (20-hectare) Jurong Bird Park. The setting for the brilliant-hued birds is in itself an attractive park. A tropical rain forest, with a waterfall plunging into a valley below, with bright flowers everywhere, and bridges spanning small streams, it sets the stage for the three thousand birds that live here. About half the birds wander freely in the world's largest walk-in aviary. Penguins waddle about on an air-conditioned "beach." Giant eagles roost on craggy walls. Birds of paradise preen their plumes to display their resplendent colors. Twice daily a bird show, with trained performers, entertains.

Tiger Balm Park

TIGER BALM PARK

The most unusual park in Singapore, of quite a different stripe from the government-run parks, is a private enterprise, the Tiger Balm Gardens. Here two Chinese brothers, Aw Boon Haw, the "Tiger," and Aw Boon Park, the "Lion," have filled a garden with amazing, colorful, often bizarre, and grotesque figures—statues that depict Chinese legends and morality tales.

Made of brightly painted cement and stone, the figures loom larger than life, an extravaganza that attracts millions of visitors. The capital used for the park came from the fortune made in the manufacture and sale of a medicinal ointment called Tiger Balm.

On the planning board for the future is the redevelopment of this park into what will be the world's first Chinese mythological high-technology park.

Singaporeans have nicknamed the war memorial (left) "chopsticks."
The half-lion, half-fish Merlin statue (right) is the city's emblem.

Chapter 7

NOTED LANDMARKS

MERLIN STATUE

The Merlin statue at the mouth of the Singapore River is the official symbol of Singapore. Standing over 26-feet (8-meters) high, it is appropriately half lion and half fish. It gazes imperturbably out to sea, spewing a fountain of water from its mouth.

WAR MEMORIAL

An unusual war memorial, erected in memory of the Singaporeans who died in World War II during the Japanese siege and occupation, is formed of a cluster of four tapering white columns. Some 230 feet (70 meters) in height, these represent the four cultures of Singapore: Chinese, Malay, Indian, and European. The Singaporeans refer to the columns as chopsticks, a fitting descriptive term.

A statue of Sir Thomas Stamford Raffles in Empress Place (left) and the Dalhousie Obelisk (above)

RAFFLES'S STATUES

Two statues of Sir Stamford Raffles stand in the city, a tribute to the man whose brilliant coup launched it. The original, sculpted by Thomas Woolner in bronze, was erected in 1887 and stands in front of the British Clock Tower adjoining the Victoria Memorial Hall.

A second statue, a copy of the Woolner one, stands on the riverfront at the point on which Raffles is believed to have first set foot on the island in 1819.

DALHOUSIE OBELISK

Near the Sir Stamford Raffles landing site is the first public monument to be erected in Singapore. It is a stone pillar modeled after Cleopatra's Needle, an ancient Egyptian pillar of stone. It is called the Dalhousie Obelisk and was built in 1850 to commemorate a three-day visit made to the island by Lord Dalhousie, then governor-general of India, who was considered an outstanding administrator of British territories in the East.

Lord Dalhousie was popular in Singapore during the colonial period because he was in favor of free trade. While he was visiting the island, he gave a large sum of money to the Tan Tock Seng Hospital, a hospital for paupers in the days when paupers in Singapore were numerous. Also, his visit was looked upon as the start of better relations between Singapore and India. For all these reasons, it was thought fitting to erect the obelisk in his honor.

THE PADANG

Padang is a term in common use in Southeast Asian towns and cities to refer to an open area that has played an important role in the municipality's history and still has a place in its life today. The term is a Malay word meaning an open space or plain.

The Padang in Singapore goes back to the city's beginning, to the time when Raffles first arrived, and it was said to be the only area on the island that was not all-but-impenetrable mango swamp. So the Padang is sometimes referred to as the birthplace of the city.

At one end of the Padang, a long and wide-open green space, is the old Cricket Club that was built by the British in the 1850s and was the center of their social and sporting life during all the years of the colonial period. At the other end is another building, constructed not long after the Cricket Club as a social-sporting club for non-Britishers living in Singapore.

The grass turf was for years referred to as the Esplanade, and

A fish-eye view of Singapore and the Padang from the Westin Stamford Hotel

here the socially prominent promenaded nightly. During the day, however, in the years prior to World War II, the field was used by British troops as a parade ground. Today parades flourish on the Padang, and it is a favorite spot for festival spectaculars.

Facing out from near the center of the Padang are two solid, imperial-looking buildings, the City Hall and the Supreme Court. Both are in neoclassic style, with Corinthian pillars. The City Hall was completed in 1929 and the Supreme Court building in 1939.

It was on the steps of the City Hall that the two famous surrenders took place during and at the end of World War II. It is also on these steps that, on Independence Day, a viewing stand is set up for reviewing the annual long and colorful parade that celebrates Singapore's independence.

The facade of the Supreme Court building is somewhat reminiscent of a Grecian temple. Atop the building sits a figure

representing Justice, flanked by other allegorical figures. Carved panels, representing prosperity secured by law, also decorate the building.

CHANGE ALLEY

Change Alley takes its name from the money changers who have plied their trade here, exchanging foreign currency for Singapore dollars, for longer than the oldest Singaporean can remember. It is a dark, crowded, covered mart with all kinds of items for sale. Some are large; some are small; but none is intrinsically of great value. There are shoes, textiles, sunglasses, perfume, costume jewelry, T-shirts, vases, figurines—you name it—on sale here, and bargaining is the order of the day.

It is said that dealers in Change Alley recognize Americans by their shirts and Australians by their shorts, and that they greet them, respectively, with, "Hey, Yank!" and, "Hi, Cobber!" It is

The Science Center

also said that at one time or another every sailor in the world visits Change Alley, leaving some of his money in exchange for trinkets for a girl in the next port.

SCIENCE CENTER

Housed in a very modern building in the Jurong area is the Science Center, a popular museum with both young and old. Some five hundred exhibits are housed here, in four special theme galleries. Science comes excitingly alive in these galleries, for there are numerous participation possibilities, with buttons to push, questions to answer, and interesting things to touch and move.

The Aviation Gallery is said to be the largest exhibition of its kind in the Asia-Pacific area. It covers the history of aviation from early balloons to recent jet airplanes. Having been exposed to the

Colonial buildings from the era of British rule

principles of flight, the viewer can even test his knowledge by tests on a microcomputer.

Of especial interest to children is the Discover Center Gallery, for here there are Crazy Rooms, the Unseen World, and the Walk-in Forest.

Human evolution and space furnish other fascinating themes at the center.

EMPRESS PLACE

An area called Empress Place could be considered the colonial heart of Singapore, for here are a number of landmark buildings representing the colonial period, their architecture speaking of British elegance.

There is a block of colonial government buildings that were

*Victoria Theatre
and Victoria
Memorial Hall*

originally the East India Company courthouse, built in 1864. There also is the majestic Victoria Theatre that was constructed for Singapore's town hall in 1862. Now this building supplies one of two auditoriums where the best of Singapore's cultural events are performed. Its "twin," the Memorial Hall, stands just to the right of an imposing clock tower, which in itself is a landmark. Memorial Hall, officially Victoria Memorial Hall, was built as a tribute to Queen Victoria in 1905. It is now the permanent home of the Singapore Symphony Orchestra which, though very young as symphonies go, has gained an excellent reputation.

A rather strange "bedfellow" in this latter building is an impressive commercial bank on the main floor. Although the decor in the bank is still reminiscent of colonial days, a modern note has been added in air conditioning!

Tourists view a sculpture in front of the National Museum

NATIONAL MUSEUM

Nearby is the National Museum. For so young a country, the collection here is extensive. The first museum items, however, were collected as early as five years after Raffles landed on the island. Some sixty years later, in 1887, the first wing of the beautiful Victorian building, which now houses the museum, was opened.

The museum collection includes history, ethnology, and an abundance of artifacts representative of the four basic racial cultures in Singapore. There is a series of dioramas presenting the history and social development of Singapore, as well as a presentation of audiovisual shows in a small theater depicting the island's history.

The most spectacular exhibit, however, is the fabulous four-hundred-piece collection of jade amassed by the Tiger Balm family of Haw Par.

An interesting artifact of a different nature is the Revere Bell, donated by the daughter of American patriot Paul Revere. It arrived in Singapore in 1843 and originally hung in St. Andrew's Cathedral.

WORLD-FAMOUS RAFFLES HOTEL

A famous early-day commercial building, still in use, is the Raffles Hotel. Before becoming a hotel, it was a "tiffin house," or tearoom, and before that, the home of a British sea captain. Then, in 1866, two Armenian brothers named Sarkie opened it as a hotel.

More than a quarter of a century later, at the time of Queen Victoria's Diamond Jubilee, it was completely rebuilt and soon gained the reputation of being the grandest hotel in Asia. The neo-Renaissance building was architecturally something of a cross between a Florentine palazzo and a French château, but it was very elegant. The rich and the famous made it their mecca, and it was host to princes and maharajas, lords and film stars, and many noted authors.

But it was not always thus. The years of World War II interrupted its happy days. First it became a refuge for the British who were fleeing the Japanese, then quarters for the Japanese army officers, and finally a center for released Allied prisoners of war. It took some years after this to restore the hotel to its original grandeur, but at length it was done, and again it became a popular spot, especially frequented by authors and Hollywood stars.

Today the main dining room is called "The Tiffin Room." The

The bar in Raffles Hotel

"Long Bar," which became famous in the early days, is still in use, and there is a "Writers' Bar" on whose walls are displayed pictures of famous authors: Rudyard Kipling, Mark Twain, Somerset Maugham, Joseph Conrad, Noel Coward, and more. These were writers who did not just "stay over" in the hotel, but who made it their home-away-from-home where they wrote some of their major works.

Inside, huge ceiling fans purr softly, stirring the tropical air. Outside, peaceful lawns, overhung by magnificent travelers palms, invite pleasant strolls.

While nostalgia is the Raffles's chief appeal today, the building itself is of sufficient note to be one of nine buildings in Singapore preserved as Historic Monuments under government order.

Still, the famous hotel's 102 years are showing, and it has by some been called "seedy" today. As a result, there has been speculation that it might be torn down, particularly since the land

Two views of the original Raffles Hotel

on which it stands is extremely valuable. Fortunately, however, it is to be given another chance. Its present owners have announced a S $27.3 million renovation soon to be undertaken, a project to be carried out in phases over a two-year period. The hotel is to remain open during the renovation.

The central block of the hotel will remain intact, but the old ballroom and the courtyard wing are to come down in order to make room for a parking garage under the building, for new "function rooms," and for a new bedroom wing.

Somerset Maugham, on one of his visits, once said the hotel "stands for all the fables of the exotic East." This is still used as the hotel's motto, and it is the expectation of its banker owners that after its current renovation this statement will still remain true of Raffles.

Singapore from the Compass Rose restaurant

RAFFLES CITY

Just around the corner and a little over a block away from the famous old Raffles Hotel is another very different monument to Stamford Raffles. A huge, extremely modern, multilevel shopping center and office building complex bears the name "Raffles City." The "city" includes Singapore's tallest hotel, which has seventy-three stories, and is called the Westin Stamford. It has 1,257 rooms and suites. It caters to conventions and large tour groups. The Westin Plaza, which is adjacent, is geared more to individual travelers. The two hotels together make available to their clientele a wide variety of sports opportunities. They provide squash courts, tennis courts, swimming pools, a Jacuzzi, and a fully equipped health club.

The Westin Stamford has the highest hotel restaurant in the world. Called the Compass Rose, it is three stories high (the sixty-ninth through the seventy-first floors) and offers a fine view not only of Singapore but also of the shorelines of Malaysia and Indonesia.

Chapter 8

TEMPLES, MOSQUES, AND CHURCHES

Because of its multiracial makeup, the city of Singapore has a variety of places of worship: Buddhist temples, Hindu temples, Muslim mosques, and Christian churches.

CHINESE TEMPLES

Among the Buddhist temples, houses of Chinese worship, one of the most unusual is the Sakaya Muni Buddha Gaya (Temple of One Thousand Lights).

In this temple is an immense statue of Buddha surrounded by myriad electric light bulbs. The seated Buddha is fifty feet (fifteen meters) in height, and with the lights blazing to symbolize a world enlightened by Buddha, it is an impressive sight.

Another Chinese temple, the Thian Hock Keng (Temple of Heavenly Happiness), is famous because of its history. It is located near the seaside where, in early days, immigrants came ashore and offered prayers of thanksgiving for their safe voyage and for their arrival in a new homeland.

Opposite page: The Buddhist Temple of One Thousand Lights

The present structure replaces a humble "joss house" (Chinese shrine) built in 1821 by grateful immigrants. The temple was erected twenty years later and was dedicated to the Chinese Goddess of the Sea, Ma Chu Poh. Her statue is among the historic relics within.

The building is ornately decorated with dragons and gilded carvings. One of its most interesting historical features is to be found in the stone pillars and sculptures, which were imported from China.

There are numerous newer Buddhist temples that have a much more modern appearance than the old, time-worn ones.

THE BUDDHIST RELIGION

Buddhism, the religion practiced by the worshipers in the Buddhist temples, teaches that right living, right thinking, and self-denial will bring the soul to Nirvana, a divine state of release from earthly difficulties.

Buddha was a philosopher and teacher who lived about 500 B.C. and founded the Buddhist religion.

HINDU TEMPLE SRI MARIAMMAN

The most spectacular temple in the city of Singapore is an Indian one incongruously situated in the heart of Chinatown. This is the oldest temple in the city, the Sri Mariamman. Its immense ornate gate, tapering skyward in the form of an inverted cone, is covered with tier after tier of brightly colored sculpted animals and saints.

The courtyard into which the gate leads is rich with carved

Sri Mariamman Temple (left) and a close-up of the statues on Sri Vadapathira Kaliamman Temple (above)

archways and the temple itself, under richly decorated domes, is a riot of colorful ornamentation.

The original temple was built in 1827, added onto until 1843, and restored in 1984. It is typical of the very elaborate Hindu religious architecture.

THE HINDU RELIGION

The Hindu religion is a religion developed from Brahmanism, but with the omission of the old Brahman caste system and the addition of touches of Buddhism.

Fundamental features of Hinduism are reverence for the sacred scriptures called *Vedas*; careful observance of various regulations regarding diet, marriage, and burial; the performance of certain rites and sacraments; and prayer. Love, duty, piety, and morality are stressed.

71

The Sultan Mosque

MUSLIM MOSQUES

Singapore is replete with mosques as well as temples. The golden domes and minarets shine in the tropical sunlight. Five times daily plaintive-sounding chanters call the faithful to prayer in the mosques.

Of the many mosques in Singapore, the Sultan Mosque is the largest and most accessible to the largest number of Muslims. Although the exterior is ornate, the vast prayer hall within is simple, its walls decorated only with passages from the Koran, Islam's holy book. At noon on Friday, the Muslim sabbath, the floor of this huge hall is covered with kneeling prayers, their white-turbaned heads looking like a garden of blooming white flowers. The Sultan Mosque was completed in 1928.

Other smaller mosques are scattered about the city.

THE MUSLIM RELIGION

The Muslim religion, called Islam, teaches that there is only one God, referred to as Allah. The founder of this religion was Muhammad, and he is considered the major prophet by followers of this faith.

CHRISTIAN CHURCHES

There also are numerous Christian churches in Singapore: cathedrals are St. Andrew's, St. Joseph's, and the Cathedral of the Good Shepherd. The Armenian church, Singapore's oldest church, is also of note. It was built in 1835 when there was a flourishing colony of wealthy Armenians in Singapore. Considered an architectural classic, its plans were drawn by George Coleman, who planned a number of the best buildings of this period. The church was built on a square plan, with four projecting porticoes and a lovely steeple topping the central square. The church is still used for regular services.

Behind the church, at the top of a steep grade known as Canning Rise, lies an old Christian cemetery. This spot, once called the Forbidden Hill, was a fortress of Malay rulers. At the entrance are wide Gothic gates made of white stone.

Besides the Christian graves, there is a Malay grave that is considered sacred by the Malays, for it is believed by them to be the burial place of the last ruler of fabled Singa Pura.

St. Andrew's Cathedral is the most frequented Anglican church in Singapore. It is a fine white, English-Gothic building, constructed between 1856 and 1861 as the replacement for an earlier church that had been damaged by lightning.

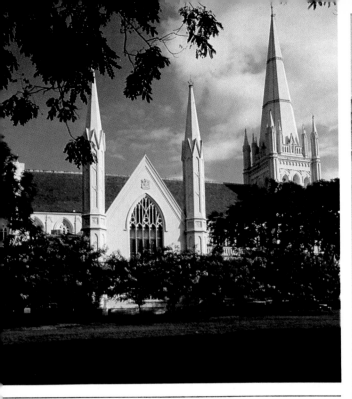

St. Andrew's Cathedral (above) and
Maghain Aboth Synagogue (right)

This cathedral is known for its beautiful stained-glass windows and for its bells that were cast by the same craftsman as the bells in Big Ben in London.

The interior of the cathedral is unusual in that it is fashioned in Indian plaster made from shell lime (lime made of crushed shells), egg whites, and sugar. This plaster, called "madras," is so hard that it is almost impossible to drive a nail into it. This early place of worship was built by Indian convict labor.

Singapore's most renowned Catholic cathedral is the Cathedral of the Good Shepherd, built in 1846. Almost one hundred fifty years later, it stands proudly, a good, solid structure, its tall steeple pointing heavenward.

There are modern Protestant churches for the worship of Baptists, Methodists, Presbyterians, and other sects.

THE CHRISTIAN RELIGION

The Christian religion, both Catholic and Protestant, is a monotheistic one that teaches that Jesus Christ was the Messiah, that he died on the cross for the sins of mankind, and that on the third day he rose from the dead. Easter celebrates the Risen Christ.

JEWISH SYNAGOGUES AND JEWISH BELIEFS

There are two Jewish synagogues in Singapore, under the guidance of one rabbi: the Maghain Aboth, which celebrated its centennial in 1979, and the Chased El, built in 1904 by Sir Manasseh Mayer.

The Maghain Aboth is a vaulted building, which sits on a rise under protecting shade trees.

The Chased El is an imposing white structure with entrance archways and arched designs above its windows.

The first Jews in Singapore settled there in 1840. They were of Baghdadi origin. It was at this time that the Sassoon family (a prominent family of Jewish merchants, philanthropists, and men of letters who had risen to great affluence and influence in England, India, and China) established business interests here.

JEWISH BELIEFS

The Jewish religion follows the precepts of the Old Testament, emphasizing the Mosaic Law, and the Talmud, which is concerned with legalistic and ritualistic matters. It does not accept the concept of Jesus Christ as the Messiah.

Chapter 9

THE PULSE
OF THE ISLAND

To characterize Singapore, such words as unified, energetic, efficient, active, colorful, and prosperous are appropriate. Neat, clean, beautiful, and *tall* are words that best describe her physical appearance.

A number of these characteristics are due to the government, in particular to Lee Kuan Yew as prime minister and the People's Action party (PAP) in whom has rested the governing power since 1959.

Under this strong leadership, the state of Singapore has taken a prominent part in affairs of the East and beyond. She is an active member of the Association of the Southeast Asian Nations (ASEAN), which also includes the powers of Brunei, Indonesia, Malaysia, the Philippines, and Thailand. With goals of accelerating economic growth among its members; developing economic cooperation in the region; encouraging social and cultural progress; and promoting regional peace and stability, this organization has proved effective. Through it, Singapore has prospered, gained prestige, and come in contact with major powers.

Opposite page: A striking view of Singapore
Inset: A fish farm that harvests ornamental fish for export

Litter-free streets and parks add to the pleasure of an afternoon stroll.

For example, after ASEAN requested Japan to reduce tariff barriers, Japan lowered tariff by as much as 20 percent on some eighteen hundred items, a move that was very beneficial to Singapore.

Also, as a member of ASEAN, Singapore became a part of an agreement on cooperation in economic development, education, culture, and control of narcotics, with the United States.

Much credit also goes to the people who, with all their ethnic differences, have lived amiably together, have worked hard, and have been obedient to law and order.

Due both to government orders and to people's compliance with them, there is no speck of litter to be seen on or along any sidewalk or street on the island. Stiff fines deter the dropping of a candy wrapper or cigarette butt. A S $500 fine is imposed on anyone caught disposing of a "throw-away" on public thoroughfares or in parks.

Construction going "up"

The towering high rises that make up most of the city give evidence both of careful planning and countless work hours in the building. However, manual labor for construction is widely imported from other Southeast Asian countries, both because such help can be obtained more reasonably than at home and because the Singaporeans prefer other kinds of jobs. As the Singaporeans express it, "We have no place to go but up," and so "up" they go at a rapid pace.

SINGAPOREANS AT WORK

Of the work force in Singapore, approximately seventy thousand are employed by the government under numerous ministries, subdivided into boards. For example, the ministry of community development runs and coordinates social service for the poor, the underprivileged, and the handicapped.

A Japanese freighter is docked in the port of Singapore.

SHIPPING AND TRADE

With international shipping and trade being the lifeblood of Singapore's economy, large numbers of workers are employed at dockside, in warehouses, and on merchant ships. (Fifteen hundred or more seamen are on board ship at any one time.) Also many men and women are employed as office workers in offices pertaining to shipping.

Beginning with 1819 when the island was opened as a trading post, Singapore has grown to be a giant in foreign trade. Its first upstart came when the sailing vessels were replaced by steamships; then in 1869 came the boon of the opening of the Suez Canal, which vastly improved shipping routes by opening a sea-lane between the Mediterranean and the Red Sea. Later the development of the tin and rubber industries on the nearby Malay Peninsula brought further trade; finally, the growth of manufacturing on the island itself increased shipping.

With all of these things in her favor, plus her strategic location and status as a free port, Singapore has become a world trade center, the base of operations for all kinds of trade. In the last quarter of the twentieth century, the value of her trade has increased fourteenfold. Singapore today ranks as the eighteenth-largest exporting country in the world, the fourteenth-largest in imports. The three nations with which she has the most extensive trade are the United States of America, Japan, and Malaysia.

A bevy of warehouses fill the port area, stacked with goods of all kinds, some from other countries and some local, awaiting ships to take them to their various destinations.

MANUFACTURING

Singapore's own manufactured goods have become an important segment of her trade. Machinery and appliances, electronic items, wearing apparel, paper products, rubber and plastic items, cement and asphalt, weapons, paint, various chemicals, and furniture are all widely exported. (Despite the remaining tropical forest on the island, woods for furniture making are imported. The native woods are not satisfactory for this enterprise.) Manufacturing has accounted for 22 percent of Singapore's gross national product (GNP) in recent years.

OIL

Because of the numerous oil refineries on the island, oil is one of the largest cargoes going out from her port. Oil refineries, both on offshore islets and on the mainland in the Jurong area, employ thousands of Singaporeans.

Oil refineries

There are five large oil refineries in Singapore, two on the main island, the other three on offshore islets. Familiar names the world over identify three of these refineries: Shell, Mobil, and Esso. The other two are the Singapore Refining Company and BP Singapore Pte. Ltd. The Singapore Refining Company is a joint venture of BP Singapore Pte. Ltd., Calrex Asia Co. Ltd., and Singapore Petroleum Company.

Crude oil for these operations is imported mainly from Saudi Arabia, Malaysia, the People's Republic of China, Kuwait, Iran, and the United Arab Emirates.

Refined products are shipped to many countries. The main markets include Australia, the People's Republic of China, Hong Kong, Japan, Malaysia, Thailand, Indonesia, and the United States of America.

RECLAIMING LAND

Land reclamation is very important, not only as a source of employment, but to the development and expansion of the city. With remaining space for going "up" at a premium, the only way the city can grow is by reclaiming areas of the sea. To do this, almost every hill, with the exception of Mt. Faber, which is needed as a "viewing point" as well as the cable car takeoff for Sentosa Island, has been cut down, and the soil that constituted the hill has been used to fill in where water once stood. Also, sand is dredged from the seabed of offshore areas. Thus new land areas are made.

About half the land that makes up Changi International Airport is an example of this kind of landfill. The reclamation work on this project took ten years to complete, at a cost of S $200,000,000.

With the hills gone, landfill is now being brought in from some of Singapore's uninhabited offshore islets.

Complete developments like Marine Square, which contains three hotels and a big shopping center, sit on man-made land.

The East Coast Park, which stretches from near the city center to the easternmost tip of the island, also is reclaimed land. With it Singaporeans have a beach stretching some 16 miles (25 kilometers), edged by a green park area, to enjoy.

Once again, credit goes to Stamford Raffles, for it was he who started this land-reclamation process for Singapore. During his brief stay on the island in 1819, he ordered the north bank of the Singapore River drained and reserved for government buildings. He then had a hill near the river dug up and the dirt dumped on the river's south bank.

TOURISM

Tourism in Singapore is a big income-generating business that furnishes employment for many people. With over three million tourists visiting the island annually, tour guides and tourist attractions are of vital importance.

The government, under its Tourist Promotion Board, trains and licenses tour guides of whom there are over five hundred, speaking, among them, twenty-six languages and dialects. It also keeps tourist attractions "alive and well." A billion dollars has been allotted for a five-year plan of revitalization and development of tourist allurements. With such monies, ethnic areas that charm visitors will be kept in repair, and where rebuilding is necessary, it will be done with careful attention to original periods and styles.

Setting up an orchid farm and spice garden as an attraction for tourists is a new project in the planning stage.

Singapore is a popular convention city. For four consecutive years in the late 1980s, she has ranked first among convention cities in Asia. On a worldwide basis, she has ranked seventh.

With eye-catching pavilions at World Fairs and prize-winning floats in California's Tournament of Roses, she attracts ever-increasing tourist and convention trade.

FINANCIAL INSTITUTIONS

Ever since Singapore's early days, financial institutions have been necessary to handle the large volume of money involved in international trade. Today 134 banks, 34 finance companies with over 100 branches, and 67 insurance firms are major employers.

A farmer weeds his vegetable crop

The largest bank, the Development Bank of Singapore, is jointly owned by the government of Singapore and private shareholders.

Singapore also has a lively stock exchange. On an average, S $31.5 million worth of trading transpires in a day.

AGRICULTURE

Agriculture, because much of the island is city, plays a comparatively minor role in Singapore's economy. Yet agriculture is important. Only about 6 percent of the island's land area is being used for farming. Even on relatively small areas, local farms are able to produce about 11 percent of the vegetables consumed by the island's 2.6 million people. This is made possible by the year-around summer climate that allows for intensive farming, with several crops being grown on the same plot in a year.

POULTRY AND PIGS

Besides truck gardens, small poultry and pig farms are to be found on the west coast.

Duck and chicken farmers generally raise their fowl in pens off the ground. In ground pens, pythons, nocturnal predators, are likely to kill the fowl.

Pig farms are being gradually phased out as they have been targeted as a cause of environmental pollution.

TROPICAL FRUIT

Fruit is raised also on small farms, sometimes in miniscule orchards or little vineyards. Favorite tropical fruits raised include durian, mangosteens, and rambutans.

Durian, a favorite of Singaporeans, known as "the king of fruit," is a large, thick-skinned, football-sized fruit covered with sharp spines. Its flesh has a texture like smooth custard.

Mangosteens are somewhat similar to oranges, but with a thick, reddish-brown rind. The pulp is segmented, sweet, and juicy.

Rambutans are small, about the size of a plum. They are egg-shaped and red in color, with a pulp that is juicy and refreshing.

Papayas, mangoes, bananas, and pineapples also are grown.

ORCHID AND ALLIGATOR FARMS

An orchid farm here and there brightens the landscape. It is one of the most profitable of the small farms, as orchids are raised for export.

Another interesting type of farm is the alligator farm, where

Alligators hatching (left) at an alligator farm (above)

great scaly reptiles flop about in muddy water pens. The alligators are bred for their skins, which are used to make shoes, purses, and belts.

HIGH-TECH FARMING

Under the government's Primary Production Department, a beginning is being made in high-tech farming. Agrotechnology parks have been established on 551 acres (223 hectares) of land, and in the next few years the plan is to develop 3,707 acres (1,500 hectares) for this purpose.

As high-tech farming grows, the expectation is that Singapore will be able to supply a much higher percentage of her own food than at present.

COUNTRY LIVING

Living conditions on the small farms are very different from those in the city. Instead of the family dwelling in an apartment, the farm family lives in a small one-story frame house, often quite dilapidated, the remnant of an early village.

FISH ENTERPRISES

Remnants of other small villages appear where fishermen live and bring in their catch from coastal waters. Floating cages are a favorite method of fish harvesting.

There are also licensed marine farms where high-value fish like grouper and sea bass are cultured. Some prawn farming also has been introduced.

In a different category of fish raising, aquarium fish are grown for export. These are a source of high revenue. In one year over S $47,000,000 of aquarium fish were sold.

Along with aquarium fish goes the raising of aquatic plants. These also constitute a large export trade with over S $46,000,000 worth sold in a recent year.

ECONOMY

Since gaining independence, Singapore has developed into a high wage, high productivity nation that has surpassed every other economic level in Asia except that of Japan. Singaporeans today produce a per capita GNP of S $6,900 a year.

Discussing Singapore's economy, Prime Minister Lee Kuan Yew is quoted as saying, "We are like a man on a flying trapeze who has let go of one swing and is now sailing through the air."

This little giant of a country seems to have prospered so spectacularly for five reasons: (1) its central geographical location, (2) a hardworking people with diverse talents, (3) a free-trade system, (4) a free-enterprise system with government support and intervention only when necessary, and (5) the general prosperity of other countries in the region.

There are no restrictions on foreign investments in Singapore, with the result that foreign money pours in in abundance. Japan, for example, invests more money per capita in Singapore than in the United States, Brazil, and South Korea combined.

This tiny island nation has more foreign reserves than Australia or Canada, a capital surplus of S $30 billion, and, next to Switzerland, the lowest rate of inflation in the world.

Over the past twenty-five years, her people have known a higher standard of living than her neighbors in Hong Kong, Taiwan, and South Korea.

During the mid-1980s, however, Singapore experienced a recession. A slump in construction, partially due to overbuilding, as with hotels, was one cause of the downturn. The number of tourists, particularly from other Asian countries that were having a recession also, fell off, thus limiting the number of hotel rooms needed. Another factor in the downward trend was the falloff in the price of petroleum.

This was not the first time, however, that Singapore's fortunes had taken a downhill slide. When the British removed their fleet from the Pacific in 1968, about 10 percent of the island's economy vanished with it.

Singapore rebounded, and now, in 1989, indications are that it is doing the same.

Traffic in Singapore
is well-regulated.
The low building
in the photo above
is a food center,
an area where street hawkers
are all under one roof.
Left: A Singaporean
boarding a bus,
the cheapest way
to get around the city.

Chapter 10

TAKING CARE
OF HER PEOPLE

Singaporeans have no difficulty in getting to work, to restaurants, to sporting events, or the theater, for public transportation is readily available. Of course, many people drive their own cars, and there are times, in the heart of the city, when there are traffic snarls as in any city. However, an interesting approach to alleviating this problem is being used. On streets indicated as "restricted zones," only cars carrying four or more people are allowed. Thus car-pooling is encouraged in the busiest areas.

Over thirty-six thousand public parking lots are operated by a division of the Urban Redevelopment Authority. Motorcyclists and truck drivers have separate facilities set aside for their vehicles.

Buses, some of them double-deckers, run on frequent schedules to and from the most distant points on the island.

A six-lane expressway, much of it bordered by bright flowers and verdant parkways, connects the east coast of the island with the west.

Overhead portion of the rapid-transit system

A mass rapid-transit system, underground, on the ground, and overhead, is in operation on the most frequently traveled routes. It is a conventional electrically-driven railway system—with no graffiti on the station walls or the cars. There are forty-one stations, fifteen of them underground, twenty-five elevated, and one ground level. During peak times, the trains run at intervals of three to four minutes. In areas around the stations, developments of various kinds, from landscaped areas to shopping centers, are being constructed or on the planning board.

Also on the planning board is extensive expansion of the line. When completed, it will link Changi International Airport on the east with Jurong on the west and the Causeway on the north with the city center on the south.

COMMUNICATION

Today's advanced telecommunications are in full swing in Singapore. Her Sentosa Island Earth Station provides direct access to over fifty countries, via Pacific and Indian ocean satellites and, through transit centers, to all parts of the world. Over 50 percent of her global communication traffic is through satellite links. Submarine cables serve as supplements and alternatives to satellite links.

Through her Coast Earth Station, Singapore also has fourteen-hour direct maritime communication with ships in the Pacific Ocean.

Singapore's national telephone network is one of the few in the world that is 100 percent automatic. With 100 percent push-button telephone sets, Singaporeans enjoy such helpful services as telebanking and automatic radio. There are over twenty-two thousand public telephones in Singapore, many housed in attractive outdoor booths.

With the installation of automatic mail sorting and processing equipment, Singapore has developed an efficient postal system operating out of seventy-six post offices. Mail is delivered twice a day in the city and Jurong Industrial area, once a day in other areas. The General Post Office, the Airport Post Office, and one other offer postal services on a twenty-four-hour basis.

On the main island, mail posted under the Local Urgent Mail Service is delivered within three hours of being posted.

The Post Office also handles several services besides mail. These are agency services for government departments and include the issue and renewal of radio and TV licenses, renewal of drivers' licenses, and acceptance of Medisave/Central Provident Fund payments.

Because of its varied ethnic population, Singapore has newspapers published in several languages. There are two English dailies, of which *The Straits Times* has been in circulation since

1845. However, the daily with the largest circulation is one of the Chinese papers, of which there are three. There are also Malay and Tamil newspapers.

NATIONAL DEFENSE

After Singapore gained her independence, she established a defense system comprised of army, navy, and air force. Now every male over the age of eighteen is required to spend two-and-a-half years in one branch of the armed services. When they have completed this service, they are transferred to the reserves, where service ends at age fifty for officers, forty for those in the ranks.

The army is the largest of the three branches, so there is a big active army base on the island. A number of vocational schools offer army enrollees specialized training.

The navy plays a crucial role in defense because of the seas surrounding the country. It has a fleet of thirty-two ships: gun boats, patrol craft and minesweepers, and support ships. Seamen receive their training at the School of Naval Training and the officers at the Midshipmen School.

The air force has over one hundred well-equipped aircraft of various types, both for combat and for surveillance.

The current army of forty thousand, not having much defense work to do, runs a cab company, a travel agency, and a department store.

POLICE PROTECTION

With some ten thousand police on duty and with stiff, enforced penalties for infractions of the law, the crime rate in Singapore is understandably low.

The island is divided into eight police divisions. From these eight districts, day-to-day crime prevention, patrolling, and the like are handled. In addition, the airport is policed by the airport police, and the waters by marine police. Traffic police are responsible for the flow of traffic and investigation of accidents on the 1,576 miles (2,538 kilometers) of roads and expressways.

Penalties for drug trafficking are severe, resulting in minimal drug-related crime. A Misuse of Drugs Act was passed in 1973, which made it an offense to traffic, manufacture, import, cultivate, or possess any kind of controlled drug. With ten to twenty years in jail and twenty-thousand dollar fines imposed on violators, few become involved with drugs. There is even a provision for the death penalty, if there is traffic in certain hard drugs of maximum strength.

CARE FOR DISABLED, ELDERLY POOR, AND NEEDY CHILDREN

There is very little welfare in Singapore, and what there is is limited to the retarded, severely handicapped, and elderly poor who have no immediate relatives.

The basic strategy of the government is to help the desperately poor, the handicapped, and the elderly by helping them to help themselves. There is, for example, a service for multiple-handicapped children under the age of twelve. There is also a hostel program for the disabled who wish to live on their own.

Although only three welfare homes for the aged are provided by the government, there are several assistance programs to make it possible for the elderly to remain in their own homes. One such program, called the Befriender Service, mobilizes volunteers to visit the elderly and to help them participate in social and recreational activities. It operates in fourteen public-housing complexes. Another, the Home-Help Service, helps elderly with housework, marketing, and other domestic chores.

There are forty-three senior citizen homes in the city that are not run by the government, but by voluntary and religious organizations. Most of these are financed by individual temples and churches.

In order to generate public interest in volunteerism, an annual Volunteers Day has been set aside, with the slogan, "We care, We Share, We Volunteer." Seminars for training volunteers are held, special events planned for their entertainment, and publicity distributed to alert the general public to the work done by volunteers.

The protection and care of children and young people who are victims of abuse, neglect, and abandonment is high on the ministry's social-service list. It manages six homes and three hostels for such children. In addition to their physical care, it supplies recreational, vocational, and educational programs for them. Aftercare is an important part of the residential care.

HEALTH CARE

In addition to hospitalization, Medisave makes available comprehensive health-care services: preventive, curative, and rehabilitative. The government health services are heavily subsidized, and they include dental services. Through dental health clinics, dental care is provided free to all schoolchildren.

Doctors, dentists, nurses, pharmacists, and midwives must be licensed to practice.

HELP FOR LAW VIOLATORS

Prisoners on parole and those on probation are provided supervision and noninstitutional treatment, with assistance from volunteers. Results are good. The success rate with probationers is about 80 percent and for aftercare cases, up to 92 percent.

PUBLIC UTILITIES

In Singapore's early days, gas was used for streetlights, but in 1945 it was replaced by electricity.

About 1940, the use of gas was extended from lighting to cooking and water heating, and is now used in one out of every three households for these purposes. It is manufactured by six plants and distributed to all major urban and suburban areas.

Electricity was first made available to the public in Singapore in 1906, and the first power station went into operation twenty years later. Today, per capita use of electricity has increased threefold since those early days. It is produced by the Ministry of Environment's refuse incinerator plant, by three oil-fired power stations, and by four gas turbines. It is transmitted through more than four thousand substations. The supply is monitored round-the-clock by computer.

Singapore's water supply comes from the rivers in Singapore and from Johore, the state at the southern tip of the Malay Peninsula. To the consumer, it comes directly from reservoirs where it is stored following its purification at treatment centers.

The water is moderately soft. It may be safely drunk from the tap at all times. It is tested frequently to make sure it meets international standards set by the World Health Organization.

A ferocious and brilliantly colored dragon in the Chinese New Year parade

Chapter 11
FESTIVALS, FESTIVALS!

Four New Years in one year? That's what Singapore boasts. However, this does not mean four *years* in one. It simply means that each of the different ethnic people has its own New Year, and that each of these falls at a different time in the calendar year. At each of these designated New Years, there is much celebrating with festivals and parades that turn the city into a brilliantly colored, exciting carnival. Fun and frolic, with much feasting, prevail.

Starting with the English New Year, January 1, followed by the Chinese New Year in February, and later by the Malay and Indian ones, Singaporeans enjoy the public holidays generated by the respective ethnic New Years.

The English New Year has the traditional Western "stroke-of-midnight" celebration. Crowds gather at the harbor to see and hear the ships send up flares and blow their resounding horns to usher in the New Year.

CHINESE NEW YEAR

The Chinese New Year is celebrated for a far longer period than the customary night-and-day of the English. Seventeen days is the official length of this celebration.

For at least a month prior to the initial date of the New Year celebration, Chinatown becomes a colorful spectacle as flower stands burst with bloom, and kumquat trees take their green and orange places on street corners and in front of shops. The floral decorations are bought by the Chinese to brighten their homes for this special season and a kumquat tree means good luck.

Much glittering gold and "Chinese red" appears in the shop windows in good-luck charms and religious symbols.

Tradition decrees that all debts must be paid before the start of the New Year. Houses must be cleaned until spotless, and often are redecorated for the occasion.

Each Chinese year is designated as the year of one of the animals of the zodiac: rat, ox, tiger, rabbit, dragon, snake, horse, goat, monkey, rooster, dog, and pig.

The New Year that opens the Year of the Dragon offers celebrations even more lavish than those of other years, for this is a very auspicious year. It is considered, for example, a good year to bring children into the world, for they presumably will be lucky.

On the Chinese New Year's Eve, family relationships are stressed, so there are many family-reunion dinners. Then during the first two days of the new year, the respect of young people for elder members of families is emphasized, and children visit the homes of their relatives. They are rewarded for their show of respect with little red envelopes containing "lucky money" and with sweets and other favorite tidbits.

During the days of the Chinese New Year celebration, there are many striking parades on the streets; there are Chinese street operas called *wayangs*, which are performed on busy corners; there are acrobatic shows. But the climax of spectaculars comes at

Incense is offered to the spirits of the dead
as part of the Festival of the Hungry Ghosts.

the close of the Chinese New Year. It is called "The Chingay Procession." It is a long, long parade with stilt walkers; huge, colorful papier-mâché representations of the animal of that year; characters from Chinese myth; elaborately decorated floats; and bands, clashing gongs, cymbals, and wildly beating drums.

OTHER CHINESE FESTIVALS

There are many other Chinese festivals during the year: the one celebrating the birthday of the Monkey God, the Dragon Boat Festival, the Festival of the Hungry Ghosts, and the Mooncake Festival. All have their special religious significance except for the Dragon Boat Festival.

MONKEY GOD FESTIVAL

On September 19, Chinese Singaporeans celebrate the birthday of the Monkey God. He is a much-revered god because he is

A youngster selects a piece of candy from an assortment of traditional New Year sweets.

believed to be able both to cure the sick and to absolve sins. His real title is Great Sage of All the Heavens. Legends similar to Western fairy tales tell of his numerous adventures.

At dusk on the evening of the Monkey God's birthday, altars are set up to hold images of him. A medium is then prepared to communicate what the god has to say to the people. Gongs and drums sound as the temple medium takes his "bath of seven colors" with vari-hued flowers strewn in the water. His bath over, the medium goes into a trance as he is led to a red dragon chair. After he does some leaping and somersaulting over the altar in the temple, devotees kneel before him and he gives each of them a paper charm.

The festival continues the following day with processions in which other mediums carry a sedan chair supposedly occupied by the spirit of the Monkey God.

Chinese operas and puppet shows are performed in the temple courtyards during this festival.

DRAGON BOAT FESTIVAL

The Dragon Boat Festival honors an ancient Chinese poet, Ch'u Yuan, who drowned himself in a protest against the evils of corruption.

The Dragon Boat Festival is a worldwide event, involving competition in rowing with participants from as far away as Australia and America. There are also entries from Europe and from many places in Asia.

Brilliantly painted boats with as many as twenty-four rowers, plus a drummer, make the waters off the East Coast Parkway sparkle like a wildflower garden and resound with a rumble of drums like thunder.

During the days of this festival, which is celebrated at the end of May, Chinese families have a special dish they eat in abundance. It is made of rice dumplings stuffed with meat and wrapped in bamboo leaves.

The connection between the Dragon Boat races and the death of the poet Ch'u Yuan lies in the fact that at the time he drowned himself, fishermen raced out in their boats to try to save him. They are said to have beaten drums and thrashed the water with their oars to scare away big fish that might attack him.

MOONCAKE FESTIVAL

Because mooncakes are a popular food item in Singapore, the Mooncake Festival is famous. This festival is held in September when the moon is full, to celebrate the overthrow of an ancient dynasty in China, the Mongol Dynasty, which ruled the vast thirteenth-century empire of Genghis Khan. In this celebration children parade the streets carrying bright lanterns with candles inside, making weaving patterns of flickering lights like so many fireflies.

The mooncakes, which are eaten in great numbers at this time, are rich, round pastries filled with a mixture of sweet red-bean paste, fruit of lotus, or melon seeds.

INDIAN NAVARATHRI FESTIVAL

The other ethnic groups on the island have their special festivals also. The Indian population celebrates their Navarathri Festival for nine days in September and October. In the Hindu temples there are performances of classical Indian music, drama, and dance.

In the Indian homes, shrines are set up to the three goddesses to whom the Hindus pay homage, and gifts are exchanged.

On the last night of this festival, there is a vast parade, with thousands of men, women, and children taking part. The focal point of this parade is a silver horse that is carried about the city from its home in one of the temples, where it is finally returned after a long ride.

THEEPAVALI FESTIVAL

The Theepavali Festival is the Hindu Festival of Lights. It is a public holiday, celebrated on the first day of November.

During the late days of October, Little India is brilliantly lighted

During Thaipusam Festival, some Indian men pierce their bodies as part of a religious ritual.

and throngs of Indians fill the streets and shops, buying special gifts, clothing, and food for the upcoming celebration.

This is a joyous festival, for it celebrates the victory of light over darkness, of good over evil.

Indian homes are lighted brightly for the occasion, and everyone dresses in new clothing, the women in shiny silk saris, the men in white *dohtis*, which are little more than loin cloths.

In the Hindu temples, shrines are decorated with flowers and the altars are piled with offerings of fruit and flowers.

MALAYS' RAMADAN

The Malays also have their festivals, the most important in connection with Ramadan, the ninth month of the Muslim year.

At the beginning of Ramadan, which inaugurates a month-long period of abstinence and fasting, activity around the mosques becomes tumultuous. Stalls are set up where favorite Malay foods will be sold after sundown. During Ramadan, the faithful Muslim cannot partake of food until after dusk. Following evening prayers in the mosques, the nearby streets become alive with celebrants.

The main celebration, however, comes at the end of Ramadan, when fasting is over, with a festival known as "The Hari Raya Pausa." The day on which this falls is a holiday. In the morning, Singapore's Muslims go to the mosques for prayers. Afterward, they visit their relatives. At night, celebrations featuring concerts and other entertainment are held in parks ablaze with lights.

NATIONAL DAY

In addition to the festivals celebrated by the various ethnic groups (two dozen of them), there is one day celebrated by *all* Singaporeans. This is their National Day, the anniversary of the country's independence.

National Day falls on August 9, and the pageantry of the day involves the military, the schoolchildren, many bands, and all kinds of entertainers, among them acrobats, clowns, and dancers. An almost endless parade through the city expresses the pride of the citizens in being an independent republic.

In the National Stadium, all seats are filled, for it is here that the show of the year culminates. It is made up of the best entertainment chosen from each ethnic group. The choices usually include dragon dances by a Chinese dance troupe and traditional Hindu dances by Indian groups.

The finale, with all of the parade participants and performers massed in colorful formation, presents a kaleidoscope of handsome dress, sparkling instruments, and multicolored flags.

Chapter 12

A LOOK AHEAD

So this is Singapore today.

What lies ahead for her?

The city of Singapore is often compared with Hong Kong, but the future paths of the two cities will not run parallel. Whereas Hong Kong goes back to China at the end of the present century, Singapore is her own mistress, and it is up to her to determine where she goes.

Physically, she has no place to go but up, and there is little land left for adding to the footing for her forest of skyscrapers—just the tiny farmlands. That leaves only further landfill as a possibility for future building sites. Some of the little offshore islands that are a part of the state are being used for industrial purposes and cannot be sacrificed for landfill. Other smaller islets have already been "mined" for fill dirt. There is the possibility of Singapore contracting with Malaysia for this essential commodity; she is only a mile away. And there is always sand that can be dredged from the sea.

At present, what the future holds for the physical growth of the little island republic is conjecture, but it appears likely that, one way or another, she will continue to "make" more land and build more skyscrapers.

Prime Minister
Lee Kuan Yew

As to the government, although there is some criticism of the paternalism of the present regime, the People's Action party still remains strong, and if and when Prime Minister Lee Kuan Yew retires, there is his son, Lee Hsien Loong.

Lee Hsien Loong, at age thirty-three, is a member of the cabinet. He is said to have both brains and flair and his father's gift for oratory. Having a liking for politics and being on the inside track, it would seem likely that he one day may be prime minister.

While he probably would lead Singapore generally in the pattern his father has set, it would appear that he might make regulations and restrictions a little less stringent. At present he gives indication of a slightly more liberal approach than his father's. An example of this is his approval of relaxing an educational rule that had determined which students could take academic courses in secondary school. With this regulation removed, all students can choose whether they will enroll in vocational or academic courses.

Today's Singaporean teenagers can anticipate a future for their homeland as being one of the most affluent countries in the world.

The government, which now owns part or all of approximately five hundred businesses, will probably not expand in this area. In fact, present recommendations suggest not only that it get into no new businesses, but also that it get out of the ones it is now in, if private enterprise will take them over.

The future thus will likely see a strengthening of private enterprise and more entrepreneurs.

ECONOMY

Barring a worldwide depression, war, or a major natural disaster, the economy of Singapore and the standard of living of her people will not only remain at today's high level, but will soar beyond it. In fact, it is said that a Singaporean who is now a teenager can anticipate that by the time he or she reaches middle age, he or she will be a citizen of the most affluent country in the world.

Boat Quay ferry terminal with the financial district in the background

If government control remains on a level even approaching that of today, crime will surely remain minimal and the city clean and beautiful.

The little farms will no doubt disappear under the pressures of expansion.

THE PEOPLE

And Singapore's people?

It is most unlikely that they will find themselves living in a welfare state, though government may expand its care for the elderly.

As today's young people often go abroad for advanced study in the professions, will "the cream of the crop" decide to adopt another country more to their liking than their homeland? Based

*Congested Singapore continues to grow
and modernize, but certain traditions will always
remain, such as Chinatown's good-luck
symbols—happiness, prosperity, and
long life—sculpted in butter (above)
for the New Year celebration.*

on present figures, it appears that there will be no great exodus.

Probably continuing intermarriages among the several ethnic groups will eventually result in a more homogenous society, but this will not occur rapidly, as each group cherishes its own culture.

Perhaps as the pace of the city increases to meet the competitive demands of the world, there will be less time for festivals. Yet surely some of the colorful pageantry will remain because of its potential for tourism.

For the same reason, Chinatown, Little India, and Arab Street will be retained as entities, at least in the foreseeable future. The same is true for the historic buildings, including temples and churches.

Colorful, Singapore will remain.

In all ways, the future of Singapore looks bright.

MALAYSIA

A
B
C
D

1
2
3
4
5
6

Johore Strait

Sorimbun Res.
Poyan Res.
Kranji Res.
Tengeh Res.
Pandan Res.
Jurong Res.

LIM CHU KANG
CHUA CHU KANG
CHOA CHU KANG
AMA KENG

KRANJI
Kranji War Memorial
Zoological Gardens
WOODLANDS
NEE SOON
SEMBAWANG
Seletar

Peirce Res.
Upper Seletar Res.
Seletar
Seletar Res.
MacRitchie Res.
Lower Peirce Res.

BUKIT TIMAH
Bukit Timah 550
BUKIT PANJANG
ANG MO KIO
SERANGOON
PAYA LEBAR
TAMPINES

JURONG
CLEMENTI
National Univ. of Singapore
PASIR PANJANG
QUEENS-TOWN
TELOK BLANGAH
Botanic Gardens
SINGAPORE CITY
TOA PAYOH
GEYLANG
KATONG
BEDOK
Bedok Res.
CHANGI
Changi International Airport

Pesek
Ayer Chawan
Sakra
Merlimau
Seraya
Ayer Merbau
Sentosa
Brani
National Stadium

Sudong
Hantu
Semakau
Sebarok
Lazarus
St. John's

Pandan Strait
Keppel Harbor

SINGAPORE STRAIT

Serangoon Harbor
Ubin
Tekong Kechil
Tekong
Tekong Res.

MALAYSIA

103°40'
103°45'
103°50'
103°55'
104°
104°05'

1°25'
1°20'
1°15'
1°10'

SCALE

Expressway
Major Road
Rail Road

0 2 4 6 Miles
0 2 4 6 8 10 Kilometers

MINI-FACTS AT A GLANCE

GENERAL INFORMATION

Official Name: Republic of Singapore

Capital: Singapore

Official Languages: Chinese, English, Malay, and Tamil (the language of southern India). At least 75 percent of Singapore's citizens speak and understand rudimentary English.

Government: Singapore has been an independent republic since its secession from Malaysia in 1965. A president serves as head of state, and a prime minister serves as head of government. The Parliament is made up of one chamber consisting of 75 members elected at least every five years.

Following the British model, the government is organized into executive, legislative, and judicial branches.

The dominant political party is the People's Action party, a moderate Democratic socialist group.

National Song: "Majullah Singapura" ("Forward Singapore")

Flag: There are two horizontal stripes—red on top, for equality and brotherhood, and white below, for purity and virtue. In the upper-left corner are a white crescent and five white stars—for democracy, peace, progress, justice, and equality.

Money: The basic unit of currency is the Singapore dollar, S $. In 1988 1 Singapore dollar was equal to 46 United States cents.

Weights and Measures: Singapore uses the metric system.

Population: Estimated 1988 population—2,669,000; 100 percent urban

Religion: Singapore is a secular state with complete religious tolerance. The main religions are Islam, Buddhism, Christianity (almost equally divided between Catholic and Protestant), and Hinduism. The population also includes Sikhs, Jews, Zoroastrians, and Jains. The Chinese are mostly Buddhist and Taoist; Malays and some Indians, Muslim; and other Indians, Hindu.

GEOGRAPHY

Highest point: Timah Hill, 581 ft. (177 m), above sea level

Lowest point: Sea level

Coastline: 32 mi. (51 km)

Mountains: The western and southern parts of Singapore island are dominated by ridges running from northwest to southeast. Almost 64 percent of the land is less than 50 ft. (15 m) above sea level.

Rivers: There is a dense network of small streams. The longest is the Seletar, which runs about 9 mi. (14 km) in all.

Climate: Average monthly temperatures are uniformly high throughout the year, varying only from 77° F. (25° C) in January to 81° F. (27° C) in June.
Rainfall is evenly distributed throughout the year, although the northeast is subject to monsoons from November to March and the southwest, from May to September.

Greatest Distances: (on Singapore island):
                        East to west: 26 mi. (42 km)
                        North to south: 14 mi. (23 km)

Area: 238 sq. mi. (616 km²)

NATURE

Trees: The central part of the island is covered with rain forests, and mangrove swamps lie along the northern coast. The destruction of the original vegetation has been vast, but more than 2,000 species of higher plants and about 155 species of ferns remain. The primary forest includes wild species of the durian, breadfruit, mangosteen, rambutan, nutmeg, and mango, and oaks with evergreen leaves.
There are many spectacular flowering trees, such as the golden angsana, various species of eugenia, several species of cassia, and the African tulip tree. The Botanical Gardens has one of the largest collections of palms in the world.

Animals: Wild animals such as tigers and leopards once lived in Singapore but are now extinct because of urban development. Little remains of the original animal life. The largest native animals are the long-tailed macaque (an Asian species of monkey), the slow loris, and the scaly anteater.

Birds: Birds are numerous, especially those that have adapted to a relationship to man, such as the Indian mynah bird, the brahminy kite (with reddish-brown plumage and a white head and breast), and the house swallow.

Fish: Marine life is diverse and fascinating. There are at least 150 species of prawns. King crabs, dolphins, green turtles, lobsters, grouper, and sea bass are common. Spanish mackerel, flatheads, anchovies, scads, and croakers are found everywhere.

EVERYDAY LIFE

Food: Restaurants offer an assortment of Chinese, Indian, and Malay dishes. A combination of Malay and Chinese dishes called "nonya" also are served in restaurants and homes.

The cultural complexity of Singapore is reflected in the dietary restrictions that prevail among its population groups: pork, the favorite food of the Chinese, is forbidden to Malays and to Indians of the Muslim faith; beef is forbidden to the Hindus, and meat of all kinds to some Indian groups.

Local fruits, vegetables, and fish account for much of the Singaporean diet: vegetables include choy san, pak choy, Chinese kale, lettuce, watercress, celery, cucumber, long bean, chili, and radish. Local fruits include banana, starfruit, mango, lemon, and papaya. A number of freshwater-fish farms cultivate carp of various varieties and prawns.

Housing: Some people live in bamboo houses thatched with palm leaves, but the wealthier sections of the city of Singapore include modern single-family homes surrounded by flowers, shrubs, and trees. Extensive suburbs are composed partly of bungalows, semi-detached residences, and apartments, and partly of rural huts made of thatched or corrugated materials. The government has built many large apartment complexes, which are part of communities called new towns.

Holidays

> January 1, New Year's Day
> Two days in January or February, Chinese New Year
> Late February, Hari Raya Haji (Muslim)
> March or April, Good Friday (Christian)

May 1, Labor Day
August 9, National Day
November 1, Festival of Lights (Theepavali)
Early November or late December, Hari Raya Pausa (Muslim)
December 25, Christmas (Christian)

Culture: Cultural activities derive from the civilizations of China, India, Indonesia, or the West. Traditional Chinese and Indian music, painting, and drama are practiced by a number of societies and professional groups. Malay music has wide appeal.

Films from Hong Kong, Taiwan, and the United States attract wide audiences.

The Singapore Science Center is the only science museum in Southeast Asia.

Some painters specialize in batik cloth, but on the whole the arts do not flourish. The art museum at the University of Singapore has a fine collection of Southeast Asian artists.

The National Theatre Company was established in 1968 as a center for amateur dance, music, and drama.

Sports and Recreation: Cricket, tennis, and football show the British influence. Waterskiing is popular also, as are golf and polo. The International Sports Complex includes facilities for a wide variety of activities.

Amateur boxing, karate, and Eastern forms of wrestling involve Singaporeans from all walks of life.

Transportation: Singapore is a major world transportation nucleus. It is the world's second-most active port (after Rotterdam). Roughly half of the ships that use Singapore as a port are engaged in trade between Singapore and Indonesia. Railroads connect Singapore and West Malaysia. Roads are numerous. The mass-transit system is excellent.

More than 20 international and pan-Malaysian airlines use Changi Airport.

Communication: Radio and television communication is good, with transmission in the four official languages. The state-owned Singapore Broadcasting Corporation (SBC) broadcasts daily on medium wave and FM. Two TV channels, two Malaysia channels, and an educational TV channel are in operation.

The press is expected to function as the government's partner, not its adversary, and journalists failing to meet this expectation have been disciplined.

There are newspapers in several languages, including two English dailies (*The Straits Times* is the larger), and three Chinese.

Telephone service and mail service are exceedingly efficient and reliable, establishing high-quality communication with the rest of the world.

Schools: The literacy rate in Singapore is high—85 percent overall and more than 90 percent for those under 35. Primary education is free for all citizens. It is taught in one of Singapore's official languages, and a second language is compulsory.

Secondary education is available in technical, commercial, and academic subjects. There are also technical institutes.

The National University in Singapore provides academic and professional courses to postgraduate levels. Separate institutes train teachers, nurses, radiographers, and seamen. There are also many centers for adult education.

Health: Deaths caused by infection and parasitic disease have been largely reduced since the 1950s by improved medical facilities and technology and better sanitation and public health measures. Conditions are generally comparable to those in advanced nations. The range and quality of medical care are notably high, and there are a large number of doctors and dentists.

The council of social service provides welfare services for the sick, aged, and unemployed.

ECONOMY AND INDUSTRY

Chief products:
Manufacturing and processing—Chemicals, electronic equipment, lumber, machinery, metals, paper, petroleum products, processed food, rubber, ships, textiles and clothing, transportation equipment
Agriculture—Eggs, pork, poultry

IMPORTANT DATES

14th century—First written reference to Singapore appears in Chinese chronicles

1811—Singapore annexed to Malay Sultanate of Johore

1819—Singapore opened as a trading center by Thomas Stamford Raffles of the East India Company

1824—All of Singapore comes under British control

1826—Singapore becomes part of the Straits Settlements; Raffles dies in England

1832—Chinese ships put an end to piracy

1920s and 1930s—British build an air base and a naval base

1942-45—Japanese flag flies over Singapore

1946—Straits Settlements dissolved; Singapore becomes crown colony

1955—Crown allows Singapore partial self-government

1959—Singapore granted complete internal self-government

1963—Singapore joins the Federation of Malaysia

1965—Singapore withdraws from Federation of Malaysia; becomes independent sovereign state

1971—152 years of British military presence come to an end

IMPORTANT PEOPLE

Aw Boon Haw, the "Tiger," and Aw Boon Park, the "Lion," two Chinese brothers who run the Tiger Balm Gardens, statuary depicting Chinese myths and legends.

Ch'u Yuan, ancient Chinese poet honored by Dragon Boat Festival

Genghis Khan (c. 1162-1227), thirteenth-century Chinese emperor

Lee Kuan Yew (c. 1923-   ), first prime minister—1965 to the present

Lee Hsien Loong (c. 1953-   ), son of Lee Kuan Yew; will succeed him; member of cabinet

Thomas Stamford Raffles (1781-1826), significant figure in development of Singapore; worked for East India Company in early nineteenth century

Tunku Long, crowned sultan of Johore, 1819; gave possession of island of Singapore to East India Company

119

Handicrafts for sale in Arab Street

INDEX

Page numbers that appear in boldface type indicate illustrations

124

ABOUT THE AUTHOR

Marion Marsh Brown grew up on a farm in Nebraska, loved her life there, and attributes much of her success as an author to those early years. Now a widow, she lives in Omaha. She has one son and three grandchildren.

For a number of years she was a professor of English at the University-of-Nebraska-Omaha, but took early retirement in order to devote more time to writing. She continues, however, to teach writing classes and to lecture at writers' conferences and seminars. She is a past president of the Nebraska Writers Guild and current secretary of the Omaha Branch of the National League of American Pen Women.

Her favorite leisure-time activities are reading and traveling. She revisited Singapore when preparing this book.

She is the author of seventeen published books, some two-thirds of them for young readers. Her previous book for Childrens Press is *Sacagawea: Indian Interpreter to Lewis and Clark.*